A CLEAN & TIDY CASE OF MURDER - A TRULY MESSY MYSTERY

AN EMILY CHERRY COZY MYSTERY
BOOK FOUR

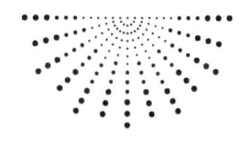

DONNA DOYLE

PUREREAD.COM

Copyright © 2023 PureRead Ltd

www.pureread.com

All rights reserved. No part of this publication may be reproduced, distributed or transmitted in any form or by any means, without prior written permission.

Publisher's Note: This is a work of fiction. Names, characters, places, and incidents are a product of the author's imagination. Locales and public names are sometimes used for atmospheric purposes. Any resemblance to actual people, living or dead, or to businesses, companies, events, institutions, or locales is completely coincidental.

CONTENTS

Chapter 1	1
Chapter 2	9
Chapter 3	18
Chapter 4	27
Chapter 5	35
Chapter 6	43
Chapter 7	49
Chapter 8	59
Chapter 9	68
Chapter 10	76
Chapter 11	84
Other Books In This Series	91
Our Gift To You	93

CHAPTER ONE

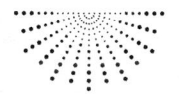

"I know it's in here somewhere." Emily Cherry opened the hall closet and caught a stack of bed sheets before they spilled out onto the floor. "Oops! Watch out!"

Anita stepped up next to her and opened the door a little bit wider. She'd come over to have some tea and a chat while they spent the long, rainy afternoon together. Thunder rumbled gently outside. "Could it be in that box down there? I think I see some other yarn peeking out the top."

Emily bent down to check, although she already knew the answer. "No, that's some heavier weight yarn that I bought for making blankets. I just want some really fine stuff that I can use to make a few cat toys for the shelter."

"Still enjoying your time volunteering over there?" Anita asked as Rosemary slipped between her feet and began sticking her paws in any little crevice she could find among the numerous items on the bottom shelf. She came up with a small round bead and proceeded to bat it against the walls, her tail flicking joyously.

"Oh, of course!" Emily enthused. She was getting irritated that she couldn't find what she needed. She simply wanted to grab a bit of yarn and a crochet hook to keep her hands busy while she and Anita talked. It was so nice to be retired, but she still liked to feel productive most of the time. She pushed aside a bag to look behind it, just in case she'd stuffed the yarn back there. "I told Lily down at Best Friends Furever that I would continue to feature a pet every week on my blog, and I figure I might as well put in some volunteer time whenever I go down there to get a photo and the story on the animal. It's nice to feel as though I'm making a difference in the lives of those sweet pets."

"Seems to me like you need to make a difference in how much stuff you have in your house," Anita replied gently. "You're never able to find anything lately."

Emily juggled the stack of sheets, which simply didn't want to stay put on their small part of the shelf, as she pushed around some more boxes and bags. "It's not that bad," she grumbled, even as she realized that she didn't know half of what had been stowed in this closet.

"I'm not saying it's bad," Anita corrected. "I'm just saying that it could be better. There are a lot of people these days who talk about home organization and what an impact it has on a person's life. Not just in terms of being able to find a jacket when they need to, either. There's talk about how it improves your mood and your general wellbeing. It's like clearing out the physical clutter cleans out the mental clutter, too."

Glancing over her shoulder at her friend, Emily pulled out a box and set it on the floor. "I don't know about that. People will say all sorts of things if they think it makes them sound important. The one thing I do know is that I'm never going to find that yarn if I don't take some of this out of here first."

"That's exactly what I'm saying," Anita agreed. She moved carefully around Rosemary as she pulled down several bags. "Have you been following Piper Hawkins online?"

"Who's that?" Emily tried to keep up with the news, but she wasn't quite as good about keeping up with trends. They were always changing anyway.

Anita slid several boxes and bags further away to make room for the ones they were still pulling out of the closet. "She's this amazing organization expert. Well, she calls herself an 'interior stylist,' but it's the same thing if you ask me. Her company has put out a few videos on what they've been doing, and it's just remarkable! They'll take this whole big, jumbled mess, get rid of a few things that aren't being used, and then have it all organized in little bins and labeled before you know it. You can find everything you need in a jiffy, without any fuss."

"Hmph. You're not supposed to believe everything you see on the internet, you know."

"Ha! Now you're starting to sound like me!" Anita laughed.

Emily grinned at that one, especially since she'd always appreciated her friend's quick wit and sassy comebacks. "Good for me. Here, you can put this box with that one over there."

"What's in all these?" Anita asked.

"Just about everything. Receipts, other bits and bobs that I just didn't know what to do with. At least some of it is in containers, but this whole shelf here is just a pile of stuff." She frowned, unsure of how to tackle it.

"Is there anything you don't want to keep? We could start a donation pile," Anita suggested.

She really hadn't meant to turn this into a project. Emily only wanted to find her yarn and sit right back down in her favorite armchair with Rosemary at her feet, playing with the little tidbits of yarn that dangled down. Now, Rosemary had shoved her way onto the bottom shelf and was digging out just as many items as the humans were. The hallway was filling up, and there was no going back unless she wanted to just shove it all back in the closet. "Yes, let's do that."

Anita headed off to grab some trash bags as well as a few empty boxes from the garage.

Emily looked down at Rosemary. "Do you think she's right? Is it really time to get rid of some of Sebastian's things?"

The cat stepped out from the little hiding hole she'd made for herself and twirled around Emily's ankle, rubbing the side of her face sweetly on her owner's leg.

"You're right. It's going to be kind of a difficult thing. I loved my Sebastian very much, and I think about him all the time. I don't suppose I really need to keep every article of clothing he ever wore just to make sure I still think about him, though. He was far more important than that." Emily had completely cleared out one shelf now, but the yarn was nowhere to be found.

Spotting a ballpoint pen that'd fallen down from somewhere higher in the closet, Rosemary laid down flat and wiggled her backside. She pounced, catching the pen in her teeth and parading in a circle to show how proud she was.

"Oh, you're right." Emily stopped her efforts as she started thinking a little more about this whole thing. "It would make an excellent blog topic. I don't know the lady Anita was talking about, but I do know home organization has become a bit of a hot subject. That means I could blog about my journey with it, as well."

"What's that?" Anita asked as she returned. She waved a permanent marker. "I'm going to label this as our donation box, but there are plenty more we can use if you want to pitch more items than just what will fit in here."

"I was just telling Rosemary, or maybe Rosemary was telling me, that I could blog about going through this closet and getting it organized. It wouldn't have to be limited to this one since I have several other spots in the house that need to be gone through. There would be almost no end of potential content, with both photos and a story." Emily could feel her own excitement for the idea starting to grow.

"That's true, and I imagine it would be quite popular."

As Rosemary trotted off down the hallway with her pen, Emily's mind was still building on the idea of what her blog would look like. "I'd still feature the shelter pets, of course. Nothing will stop me from that, no matter what else I'm writing about. And Rosemary is such a big hit, I wouldn't fathom excluding her from it. Knowing her, she'll be right in the mix of it all anyway."

Anita smiled. "I take it that means you've decided it really is time to let some things go."

"It is," Emily confirmed. "What did you do with all of Dan's things when he died?"

"Well, since the neighborhood wouldn't approve of me burning them all in the front yard, I took them to a charity shop," Anita replied as she whipped open a trash bag and hung it from the bathroom doorknob so it would be ready when they needed it.

Dan had never been a very nice man, and he'd drunk himself to death. Emily couldn't blame Anita for wanting to dispose of as many memories of him as she could. While she couldn't deny there was still some sadness in her own heart, she had the benefit of being able to look back on her marriage with Sebastian with fondness. "A charity shop is a nice idea, and I think Sebastian would've like it as well. Let's start with this. It's a box of his old books, but they're not ones that were special to him. I think I'll still want to keep a few mementos, so the most significant items will need to stay."

"Of course." Though Anita's marriage hadn't been a good one, she had plenty of respect for what Emily and Sebastian had shared. "You know, you really should go online when you have a moment and check out that Piper Hawkins. The name of her business is The Happy Home. People can hire her to come and redo their whole homes for them."

"That's an interesting job, just rooting around through other people's things," Emily commented, not sure how comfortable she felt about the idea of someone doing just that in her own home. "At the very least, though, she might serve as a great consultant. I could set it up as an interview for the blog, and it might pull some more traffic in."

Anita reached up and stopped a pile of old sweaters from falling down on their heads. She carefully lifted it down and handed it over to Emily for her to go through. "Did you ever find a way to monetize your blog?"

"Now you sound like Nathan," Emily scolded with a laugh. "I haven't, but that's never been what it's about for me. I'm just getting my courage together with writing so that someday I can write a book. Or at least that's what I tell myself. Maybe I just like to blog!"

CHAPTER TWO

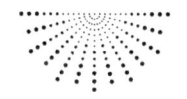

A week later, Emily stepped through the front door of Little Oakley Realty. She couldn't remember the last time she'd been in a realty office, considering how long ago it'd been since she and Sebastian had purchased their home. Several desks were arranged throughout a large room, with spaces of open floor in between them. With hardwood floors and built-in cabinets, the place felt much warmer and more comfortable than most of the modern office spaces Emily had been in. What detracted from it all, however, was the fact that there seemed to be piles of things everywhere. Stacks of folders sat on the floor next to desks. Office supplies were scattered here and there, and the wires for the computers and phone lines added to the mess.

"Can I help you?" The woman at the desk closest to the door pressed her hand over the phone and looked at Emily impatiently.

"I'm here to meet Piper Hawkins. I was invited to observe her here today." Emily had been pleasantly surprised by how willing the home organization guru had been to schedule an interview with her, considering her blog took up only the tiniest corner of the internet and surely got hardly any traffic compared to what Piper was doing on her own. She'd been even more surprised that Piper had invited her to come witness her perform one of the miracles she was becoming known for. It had all been arranged through Piper's secretary. Now that she was here, Emily could certainly tell that Little Oakley Realty needed some help.

The woman nodded curtly toward a chair. "You can wait there. They should be here soon."

Emily hardly had a chance to sit down before the front door burst open. A tall, slim woman in a black dress stood there in the entryway. She whipped off her sunglasses to reveal her striking makeup as she looked around. "Yes, I can see that this place needs me. We'll have to start by seeing what kind of storage space is available. Samantha, you start looking through the cabinets and taking stock of what they're already being used for. Kyra, we're going to need lots of bins and boxes from the van. Organize as we purge, that's my motto. But you know that, so get going."

There was no doubt this was the famous Piper Hawkins, and already she was nothing like Emily had imagined. She'd have thought her to be more of the happy homemaker type, smiling and laughing as she gently chided a customer on just how many pairs of shoes they'd decided to keep in their small closet. Still, she was here to do an interview, and so she stood up. "Ms. Hawkins, so nice to meet you. I'm Emily Cherry. I spoke with your secretary earlier in the week."

Piper whipped her head around toward Emily as she spoke and narrowed her eyes. Her face completely transformed into a wide grin and friendly eyes as soon as she understood who Emily was. "Oh, yes! So very nice to meet you. Please forgive me. I was expecting someone a bit younger for a blogger."

"That's quite all right." Emily resented the comment a little bit, but she did understand. "I really do appreciate you taking some time out of your busy schedule for me. Perhaps we could start by talking about what inspired you to start this business?" She had a pen and paper ready to go.

"Samantha, start emptying that cabinet right away," Piper ordered, going so far as to point her finger at her employee. "Nora, you help her. Check out the dimensions of it and see if it would be better for office supplies or for files, since there's obviously a paperwork problem here as well."

Emily frowned, noting that Piper hadn't introduced herself to the people working here or bothered to keep her voice down, considering they were on the phone. "Doesn't it disturb the employees to have you in their workspace during office hours?"

"One question at a time, my dear!" Piper chided with a laugh as she strutted forward through the office, angling her pointed jaw one way and then another as she looked over the space. "I don't work on the weekends, and if we kicked everyone out, then they'd never get anything done. That's simply not efficient. Kyra, make sure you get the labels right this time."

Emily scurried after her, realizing this wouldn't be nearly as easy of an interview as she'd imagined. The only part that might help was that Piper was more interested in observing and ordering her workers around than she was in actually diving into a drawer or a closet and doing the work for herself.

"As for your other question," Piper said as she frowned at Kyra, "I never meant to start up a business like this. I simply wanted a better space for myself. I was inspired while I was looking for something else entirely, and I came across the coffee mug I'd made in summer camp when I was a child. It was a very special summer for me that meant a great deal to me, and yet that coffee mug had been stored away for decades. I knew it deserved a special place, as do all the things that are truly important. The rest is just clutter. Once I realized how much of an impact that thought process had made on my life, I knew I just had to share it with others."

"I see. That makes a lot of sense." It wasn't too dissimilar from what Emily was going through herself, although she couldn't imagine doing it for other people. She was barely able to do it for herself. "And have you found it difficult to be a female business owner?"

"That's good, Samantha. Office supplies are perfect in there." Piper flashed Emily another smile, but it didn't quite meet her eyes this time. She pulled over the blonde woman she'd referred to as Nora and wrapped her in a big bear hug. "It would've been completely impossible without my best friend, Nora! She's been at my side the entire time, and she's one of my best employees. Nora, this is the woman I was telling you about who's interviewing me for a blog."

Despite the over-the-top gesture of affection, Nora made a face as her boss squished her into her side. "Nice to meet you," she said meekly.

"You, too."

A loud, jangling sound split through the office space, and Piper immediately let go of Nora to yank a phone out of her purse. "This is Piper. Excuse me, I have to take this."

"Of course." Emily stepped to the side while Piper strode toward the front doors.

She didn't go outside, however. She simply stood there at the front entrance, her phone pressed to her ear, and carried on her conversation just as loudly as she'd been speaking to her staff. "What do you want this time, Damian? No, I don't really have time to talk, especially when you consider we already worked out all the terms in court. That was what all those lawyer fees were for, you know."

Nora glanced at her boss, looking embarrassed. When it came to looks, she seemed to be the polar opposite of Piper. Her dark blonde hair was pulled into a simple braid at the back of her neck, and her makeup was subtle, with just a hint of color on her lids and pale pink lipstick. She wore the uniform of a raspberry-colored polo and khakis with sensible shoes instead of a glamourous black dress and an updo.

"I'm so sorry," Nora said, clasping her hands in front of her. "Piper is a very busy woman. You're more than welcome to join us as we get started, though. We've already talked with the manager of this office extensively, and I was able to come in about a week ago and see what we would be working with. We know that office supplies are one of the main problems. The employees need a good way to store new inventory quickly and efficiently, as well as finding what they need when they run out."

Emily nodded, glad to see that this wasn't nearly as spur-of-the-moment as Piper had made it look. "I see. And is there any reason that this cabinet is better than another for office supplies?"

Nora smiled pleasantly. "A lot of it has to do with the dimensions of the space versus the dimensions of what you're storing. You see—"

"I didn't ask you if you *liked* paying alimony," Piper snapped into the phone. "I'm not going to be one of those pushover ex-wives who's more concerned about being independent than in getting what she deserves. You'll keep paying until one of us is dead, and *that's* when you can stop worrying about it!" She tapped the screen soundly to hang up and returned to Emily. "So sorry about that. Now where were we?"

"I was just explaining about how we decide where to put things," Nora supplied. "For instance, this cabinet doesn't have adjustable shelves, and they're all fairly close together. That makes it perfect for things like rolls of tape, extra pens and pencils—"

"Yes," Piper interrupted, "and then it's also incredibly important that we create a system that's easy to maintain. It might look nice if you just stack it all into neat rows, but inevitably something is going to get knocked over and pushed around. The next thing you know, it's all completely undone. That's why we use these little plastic containers. Kyra!" Piper had just picked up a long, skinny plastic bin filled with pencils.

"Yes?" Kyra dropped what she was doing and came rushing over. She pushed up her glasses on her nose as she looked at her boss with wide eyes. "What can I do for you, ma'am?"

Piper shook the container, making the pencils rattle around inside. "What's in here?"

"Pencils."

"And what does the label on the end say?"

Kyra squinted at it and then her shoulders sagged. "Tape."

Piper shoved the box of pencils at Nora, but her eyes were blazing at Kyra. "How many times are we going to go through this? You make mistake after mistake, and you expect everyone else to come behind you and fix it."

"It's not that. I just made two labels at once to try to be efficient, and then I mixed them up," Kyra pleaded.

"It's not exactly efficient when it has to be redone, is it?" Piper snapped. "You're fired, Kyra. I'll find someone else who's willing to do the job if you aren't."

Poor Kyra opened her mouth, but she either chose not to argue or decided it wouldn't be worth it. She turned on her heel and headed out the door.

Emily watched her go, having a hard time believing she'd just witnessed that. She could understand an employee getting fired for not doing their job properly, but it'd seemed like a simple mistake. Even if it wasn't, Piper should've waited and done the firing behind closed doors.

The interior stylist, however, didn't seem bothered in the least by what she'd just done in front of an entire office full of people, no more than she'd been bothered about discussing the terms of her divorce. "Now then, what other questions can I answer for you?"

CHAPTER THREE

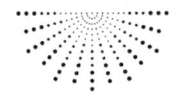

"Gran!" Lucy and Ella barreled in the front door and wrapped their arms around their grandmother.

"I'm happy to see you, too!" Emily replied as she pulled them in for a warm hug. She loved her children, but there was something special about having grandchildren. Lucy and Ella were dear to her heart, and it touched her to know they were always genuinely happy to see her.

"What's happening here?" Matthew, their father, gestured at the stacks and piles that were strewn all over the living room. "Having a rummage sale?"

Phoebe looked at Emily with equal curiosity. "Is everything all right, Mom?"

"Oh, sure. You just make yourselves comfortable, or at least as comfortable as you can. I know there's not much room in here. I'll explain everything once the others arrive."

"I think I saw Nathan and Genevieve pulling in right behind us," Matthew commented as he peeked through the front curtains. "Yep, there they are. And Mavis is parking in the street."

"Good. Let me just pull the muffins out of the oven." Emily moved into the kitchen, where Rosemary was sitting on the floor and sniffing the air. "Are they just about done, dear? Do you think you like blueberry?"

The cat slowly squeezed her eyes at her owner in pleasure.

"The girls are here, you know. I'm sure they'd want to see you."

Perhaps they'd heard Emily, because just then Lucy and Ella began calling for Rosemary. "Here, kitty, kitty!" Rosemary took off to go find them, knowing she'd get more than her fair share of pets and loving.

Meanwhile, Emily took the muffins from the oven and arranged them on a plate so she could serve them warm. She brought them out into the living room along with some tea just as the others came in the door.

Nathan looked the most alarmed. "Mother, is everything all right?"

Genevieve, always stylish and a bit snobby, tented her delicate fingers over her collarbone. "My goodness!"

Mavis was the only one who didn't seem the least bit concerned. She ran her hand over one of Sebastian's wool blazers draped across the back of an armchair and smiled. Then she raised her head and spotted the tray. "Oh, muffins!"

Emily moved a box onto the floor to make room for herself. "I'm glad you all could come today. Have a seat."

Nathan brought two chairs in from the dining room and made sure his wife was seated before he was. "Mother, I don't know what's going on here, but I'm a little concerned."

"Well then, just give me a chance to tell you about what this is, because this mess is exactly why you're all here today." Emily straightened her back and lifted her chin. "You all know it's been a while since my Sebastian has been gone. I've come to realize that there's simply too much stuff in this little house, and it's time that I started going through it and getting reorganized. After all, I don't want to leave you with all of this to deal with when I pass away."

"Don't talk about that, Mom!" Phoebe ordered. "We have a long time before that happens!"

"I certainly hope so," Emily agreed, but she pursed her lips against reminding them that she certainly hadn't thought Sebastian would be gone as quickly and suddenly as he was. "At any rate, the first step of this is to go through all of his things. There's simply no reason to keep it all, but I wanted to give you each a chance to look through it and see what you might want for your own little reminders of him. This goes for all of you," she reminded them, pointedly looking at Matthew and Genevieve. "You may have married into the family instead of being born into it, but you were all very important to Sebastian."

"Are you keeping anything?" Mavis asked as her eyes calmly scanned the room.

"Of course. I've pulled out some things like his favorite suit and his pocket watch, and of course I have his wedding ring." She'd also found some of their old love letters, a few of his favorite books, and a few other little tidbits that she knew he'd treasured. Emily hadn't yet figured out what she was going to do with them, but they'd be much easier to store now that she'd reduced it to a much smaller amount.

"I always loved this hourglass." Mavis picked up the heavy glass bauble and turned it upside down to watch the red sand fall down into the bottom. "He always kept it on his desk when he was working on something at home, and he'd give himself a break when it ran out. I remember peeking into the den to check the hourglass until I could go ask him to play in the yard with me. You mind if I take it?"

"Not at all," Emily replied honestly. She'd had a feeling one of them would want that.

Phoebe tapped her fingers on her chin. "This is hard. I want to take all of it."

"Take whatever you want," her mother encouraged.

"But I have to have the room for it, just as you're trying to make sure you're doing for yourself," Phoebe reminded her. "I think I'd like one or two of his flannel shirts. I remember him wearing them on the weekends." She got up and began going through a pile of clothing.

"Can we pick something, too?" Lucy asked, her blue eyes bright.

"I was hoping you would," Emily said with a smile. The girls were little yet, and they hadn't had as much time to get to know Sebastian, but it was only right that they should have a keepsake of their grandfather. "Go ahead and look around."

Matthew cleared his throat. He hooked a finger in the front of his collar and pulled it away from his neck. "Have you gone through anything in the garage yet? Like his tools?"

"Oh." Emily's eyes widened as she realized her oversight. "I haven't, actually. I've just been looking through all the closets and under the beds."

"Well, um, if you don't mind…" His face reddened as he trailed off a bit. "I had some pretty nice times with him when we were working on cars together. I thought it might be nice to have a wrench or two, something small.

I've got plenty of my own tools, but this would be different."

Emily wanted to get up, run across the room, and embrace her son-in-law. He was a man's man and a mechanic, the kind of guy who didn't show a lot of emotion unless it came to his wife and children. She'd always known that he was far deeper and kinder than he chose to show on the outside, however, and she loved him for it. That was exactly why she didn't embarrass him by getting up and hugging him as she wanted. "Why don't you go on out there and see what you can find?"

"Thanks." He grabbed a muffin as he headed for the garage.

Nathan sighed as he picked up a coffee mug. "Dad used to drink out of this every morning before work. Are you sure you want to get rid of it?"

Emily smiled. There were some things she'd set out in the living room not because she wanted to get rid of them but because she knew someone else would probably want them. The coffee mug was one of them. "I think it would have a wonderful home in your kitchen."

Genevieve had been sitting in her chair, watching with reserve. She'd been quiet enough that Emily wasn't sure if she were going to choose anything for herself, but now she got up and walked across the room to a small, framed print of a Van Gogh. "This was from the trip to the art museum. It was the first time I met Sebastian, and I liked him right away. This would look nice in my office, if it's all right."

"Absolutely." Emily smiled. Her heart was warm and comfortable in knowing that the love she had for her husband had been shared by all of them. If Sebastian could see all of this right now, he'd surely be just as happy as she was.

Nathan scooted forward on his chair. "What are you going to do with the rest of this?"

"I'll load it all up and take it to the charity shop," Emily explained simply. "It will probably take a few trips, since I'm sure it won't fit into my car all at once, but I'll take it a bit at a time when I get out to go to the grocery store or the animal shelter."

He shook his head. "Some of these items might bring in some money for you if you sell them instead. You shouldn't let that opportunity go to waste."

Nathan was always all about money. It was that sort of thinking that'd made him the young professional that he was, and as a marketing consultant she had no doubt that he knew exactly how people liked to spend their money, but that didn't mean she wanted to go that route. "I'd much rather not have to put all the time and struggle into it."

"It's really pretty easy to list a few things online," he countered. "You can take some photos with your cell phone, and there are several websites that are great for just this sort of thing."

Emily nodded. "Yes, I'm sure you're right. But then I have to pack it all up and mail it out or make arrangements to meet with someone in a safe place downtown. I have too many other things I'd like to do, so I'm not going to bother with it."

"But you're practically throwing money away," he pressed.

"Nathan." She looked at her son, giving him the same firm stare she'd used when he was a teenager and he insisted he knew more about paying the household bills than she did. "I understand you don't want me to shortchange myself, but I'm not interested. I've already made this decision, and I think your father would approve of it. He'd like the idea of his old things going to benefit charity. If you're that determined that the items get sold instead of donated, then you feel free to take them and sell them, but I'm not going to."

His mouth turned into a hard line, that stubborn look that always suggested he was going to dig in a little further until he got his way. Then Genevieve gently laid her hand on his arm and gave him a soft look, and his shoulders visibly relaxed. "All right. If you say so."

"Thank you." She didn't want to argue with Nathan, but she'd noticed that her son worried over her more and more as she got older, especially now that she was a widow. It was true that life was harder this way, but she was still perfectly capable of living it. "Anybody want anything else?"

"Look at me!" Ella giggled. She was enveloped in one of Sebastian's old blazers, which came all the way to her feet and barely stayed on her narrow shoulders. "I'm Grandpa!"

"No, I'm Grandpa!" Lucy had put on a pair of his loafers and a felt hat. She crooked one finger under her nose. "See, I have a mustache, so you know I'm a grandpa!"

"Girls," Phoebe turned around from the stack of shirts she was sorting, ready to scold her children, but she burst out laughing. "You look adorable!"

"Is that any way to talk to your father, young lady?" Lucy scolded.

Emily was laughing so hard now she thought she might fall off the sofa. It'd been hard to pull out all of these items, ones that Sebastian had curated over his lifetime and that still smelled of him. Seeing how it all brought the family together, however, had made it all worth it. "Looks to me like you girls have found some new items for your dress-up trunk."

CHAPTER FOUR

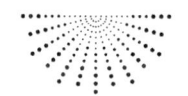

"What do you think, Rosemary?" Emily stood back and looked at the hall closet. She'd taken all of Sebastian's things out, as well as quite a few items of her own that she no longer needed. One trip had already been made to the charity shop, and her car was loaded up for the next one. That was progress, certainly, but when she looked at the closet where this whole project had started, she wasn't so sure.

The few little decorative bins she'd picked up in imitation of what she'd seen on all the other organization blogs and posts online only went so far. They didn't reach the full depth of the shelves, which meant the space behind them was wasted. Then there was a matter of choosing what items should go into what bins. It sounded easy enough, but Emily was having a terrible time deciding how this should all be done.

Rosemary must not have minded it too terribly, because she hopped on the bottom shelf and nestled herself down behind the bins.

"Not very helpful," Emily laughed as she scooped the cat back out of the closet and shut the door. "I think I might need some real help, though."

The cat trotted after her as she headed for the kitchen, probably hoping for a treat.

"Not right now, dear. I'm just coming in here to find something." Emily dug through her purse and scanned the kitchen counter. She looked over the various bits of paper she'd posted on the fridge with magnets, but it wasn't there, either. "My goodness! I guess I'll have to do a lot more organizing before I actually manage to fix this problem! Ah, here it is. Right on the kitchen table."

Emily picked up the business card Piper Hawkins had given her just before she'd left Little Oakley Realty. "My email address is on there. Be sure to send me the link to the interview when you get it posted. Or drop by if you decide you'd like to enlist my services. I'll give you a fair price."

Sighing, Emily looked at the address. She hadn't yet posted the interview, but some of that was because she hadn't been able to decide exactly how she wanted to portray the local media's hottest thing. Piper and her crew had undoubtedly made a huge difference in the workspace for the employees at Little Oakley Realty, but during that time she'd been snarky, hateful, and had fired someone. She hadn't done much of the work herself beyond labeling a few bins and pointing her finger. On a personal level, Emily didn't think Piper Hawkins was all that great. That made it difficult to decide exactly how she wanted to spin this interview.

When it came to organizing, though, she'd completely blown Emily away. By the time they'd left, all the office supplies were arranged, labeled, and handy. They'd found more space for the numerous files floating around the office, which cleaned up the desks. The various wires that snaked through the place had been bunched up with Velcro strips and carefully hidden behind and underneath the furniture. It looked like a completely different company had moved in, and Emily couldn't deny how much more appealing the office now was.

"I think that means it's time for me to do the same." Emily glanced at the weather, deciding that the thunderclouds in the distance would hold off long enough for her to get to her destination without getting caught in a downpour. She grabbed her jacket and headed across town.

The little building looked more like a house than an office, which only made sense for a business called The Happy Home. A large picture window took up most of the front wall, with neatly landscaped flowers blossoming just beneath it. More flowers lined a curved path toward the front door, where a swag of daisies hung against the pink paint. A small sign underneath the daisies read 'Open!

Please Come In!' in careful cursive, and Emily did just that.

She found a reception desk along the front of the entrance, but nobody was sitting at it. The floral wallpaper and the pale pink carpet continued the charm of the place. Emily looked for a bell on the desk, but she didn't find one. "Hello?"

When there was no answer, she dared to move past the receptionist's desk to peek into an office over on the right. "Hello?" In here she found yellow striped wallpaper and a bookshelf that'd been arranged by the colors of the covers, but again nobody was in the office.

Thinking that this wasn't a particularly welcoming reception for potential customers, Emily moved on through. She found another empty office, this one decorated in blue, and a storage closet that would make most retailers jealous. At the very end of the hallway was a door with Piper's name emblazoned on a gold plaque. The door was closed, so she lifted her hand to knock.

Once again, there was no answer. "Hello? Piper?" Emily knocked a little harder. She felt rude, but it was also rather rude for the one person in the office to have her door shut and not be responding to clients who might be coming through the door. Emily turned to walk away, reasoning that perhaps this meant she didn't need to spend her hard-earned savings on a professional organizer. Her home might not look nearly as nice if she did it herself, but she could certainly make progress.

Then she thought about Anita. The two of them had been best friends for a long time, and Emily had always admired how bold and direct Anita could be. She didn't hold back on what she thought, especially if she felt someone needed to hear it. If Anita were here with her, she would most likely strut right in that room and give Piper and earful.

That's exactly what Emily did. She grabbed the doorhandle tightly and twisted it before she could convince herself not to. The door swung open to reveal a room that felt much more modern than the other offices she'd seen thus far. The walls were painted a warm gray with a stark white trim, and a series of black-and-white photos hung in a cluster behind a large gray desk. White cubes on the left side of the room served as bookshelves, each cube holding one or two books and a knickknack. A matching cube hung directly behind the desk and presented a slightly lopsided coffee mug. Emily recognized it immediately as the one Piper had referred to when they'd met before.

There were two other things that stood out in the room. The first was that it was unoccupied. A cushy, upholstered chair had been pushed in behind the desk, but nobody sat in it. The second thing was that the desk was far less orderly than she'd have expected from someone who tidied people's homes for a living. Papers, photos, and folders were scattered across the surface, partially obscuring the computer's keyboard and mouse. Several pens and pencils peeked out of the mix. A coat rack over on the right was cluttered with jackets, sweaters, and scarves, with some of the hooks overburdened to the point that they looked like they might break at any moment.

Emily put her hands on her hips. "Well, how do you like that? I come all the way down here and they've left the office abandoned. I guess they must be out working somewhere, but still." She turned to go when she noticed something next to the desk. Emily tipped her head to the side, seeing that it was a lone black pump. How strange that Piper would leave one shoe laying out all by itself! But then Emily realized that it wasn't a simple shoe all by its lonesome. The foot that it belonged to was nearby, and as she dared to lean around the corner of the desk, she saw that the office wasn't unoccupied at all.

"Piper? Ms. Hawkins?"

Piper lay on the floor with one arm thrown over her face. Emily already had a horrible bubble of dread building in her stomach, but she leaned down and touched her wrist. The poor girl was dead, and there was no doubt of it. Bumping her hip on the corner of the desk in her haste to get back out of the office, Emily fumbled for her cell phone and immediately called the police.

They arrived quickly in a racket of sirens and lights that contrasted sharply with the pleasant atmosphere that The Happy Home had otherwise created in the building. Emily was sure not to touch anything that she hadn't already touched, and she was glad when she saw Alyssa's familiar face come through the door.

"Mrs. Cherry!" she exclaimed as she rushed to Emily's side. "What are you doing here?"

"My original plan was to hire an organizer," she replied with a frown and a shudder. "It seems that what I was actually doing here was finding a dead body."

More officers and a couple of paramedics moved past them into the building. "I'll have to ask you some questions right here in the foyer, if you're comfortable enough. I don't want to contaminate anything, but it looks like it would be a bad idea to go outside."

"Raining already?" Emily turned to look out the window, but the thunderclouds were still hovering on the horizon. Instead, she found that several people had gathered on the pavement across the street, pointing at The Happy Home and talking to each other. Several of them were holding up their cell phones. "What's going on?"

"This." Alyssa spread her arms to indicate the crime scene. "Piper Hawkins came out of nowhere and built herself a huge reputation. She's been on every local news channel, in every paper, and on countless websites. She's a local celebrity, and all the police cars out front have clued everyone in that something big is happening here."

"If those are her fans," Emily said as she glanced over her shoulder toward Piper's office, "they're going to be very disappointed."

CHAPTER FIVE

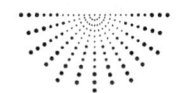

"All right. Yarn can go in this basket, then. No, Rosemary. You have to leave it in there. I know it looks like a toy because I tossed it, but I'll never make any progress if you carry it all over the house." Emily gently removed the skein of pale blue yarn from Rosemary's teeth and put it where it was supposed to go. "Although, do you think I ought to organize it further than that? Should I put all my yarn in one basket, or should I split it up by weight? Or color? Oh my, this is so much harder than I thought it would be!"

Emily chucked another ball of yarn after the first, figuring that at least if all the yarn were in one spot, then at least she'd know where to find it. Rosemary didn't seem too upset about the idea, and she occupied herself by putting her little paws up on the side of the basket and peeking inside every time

Emily tossed another bit of yarn in.

The doorbell rang, and Emily hoisted herself up off the floor. "Now don't you take anything back out of that basket," she admonished her cat, waving a finger but knowing she'd never dole out any punishment beyond taking the yarn back. "I've been working hard, and there's no point in undoing what little headway I've already made."

Emily opened the front door to find Anita standing on her stoop, lightning slashing across the sky behind her. "Get me in out of this awful weather!" her friend exclaimed as she shook out her umbrella and propped it up in the corner. "It's just terrible out there!"

"Then what are you doing out in it?" Emily asked, helping Anita out of her bright red raincoat.

"Would you believe I got bored, sitting around and watching the rain splatter on the windows?" Anita patted her snowy hair to make sure it hadn't been blown about too much. She held out a package of colorful labels. "Besides, I picked these up for you the other day and I thought you might be able to make use of them, now that you'll have to do all the hard work yourself."

"Oh, thank you! They're just what I need. Actually, what I really need is to be able to make a decision. I started off putting all my yarn in this little box. Then I realized it was too small, and I had to transfer it to another one. That's well enough, I suppose, but now I don't know what to put in the smaller box." She gestured in frustration at the items that were now scattered around on her floor. "I started all of this to have a cleaner house, but I'm afraid all I'm really doing is making a mess."

Anita fisted her hands on her hips as she studied the craft supplies. She then bent down and began loading up one of the smaller boxes with an assortment of spools of thread. "You're overthinking it, dear. You just put it together and go with it. If it doesn't work, you can always change it later. I'm sure even the professionals have to go through a bit of trial-and-error."

"It's not as though I have any way to ask now," Emily returned, feeling somewhat guilty for finding Piper's body a few days ago. "With all the articles in the paper memorializing her, though, you'd think she'd founded the city."

Anita sighed and nodded in agreement as she took a spool of thread back from Rosemary. "I need that, dear. Thank you. And I did see that. I'm just glad they didn't mention your name. They say there's no such thing as bad publicity, but I'm not sure I agree."

"I don't think I have enough readers to worry about publicity," Emily noted as she loaded up the markers that she kept for Lucy and Ella into a long, skinny box. "More than I used to, of course."

"You'll potentially have even more coming to you once you publish that interview. It was likely the last one that Piper gave before she passed away," Anita pointed out.

Emily rocked back on her heels, feeling as though she'd just been hit over the head with all the craft supplies she'd taken out of the closet. "My goodness. You're right. I'm not sure what I should do about that, then."

"Whatever do you mean?" Anita opened a small bag of loose beads and began sorting them into a container. "It'll bring you all sorts of traffic, given how much attention the papers have been giving it. You could make Nathan the happiest son in the world and do something to monetize your blog just before you put it up."

Though her statement was meant to be amusing, Emily wasn't sure she saw the humor in it. "I don't want to profit off someone's death. More importantly, I don't want it to *look* like I'm trying to profit off someone's death. I might not write it up at all."

Anita nodded. "That's up to you, of course. I wouldn't blame you, either way. It's your blog, and it ought to be whatever makes you happy."

"I just wish that all of this was making me happier." Emily waved an impatient hand at the craft supplies. "Piper believed that a clean and organized home would clear out the clutter in your mind, but I feel that it's only adding to it. I now have a To Do list that feels a mile long, and every day I wake up and think about how I can possibly check the most things possible off of that list. It just doesn't seem to end, and at the rate I'm going I feel like I'm going to end up on one of those TV programs about people who can barely move through their house because they have so many things."

Anita tossed her head back and laughed. "Now I *know* you're overthinking it! You weren't one of those people to begin with, and you're definitely not one of them now. Sure, you have a few things scattered about at the moment, but you've already gotten rid of quite a bit that you've taken to the charity shop."

"There's still this pile over here." Emily glanced at the stack on one end of the sofa. "I should feel good about it, but now that I've made the decision to donate it, it's like I can't get it out of here fast enough."

"Then let's take it out to the garage and load it in your car." Anita pushed herself up off the floor with what looked like relative ease for a woman of her age and held her hand out for Emily. "Come on. We'll do it right now, and then it'll be ready for the next time you go somewhere. Plus, you won't have to feel as though it's cluttering up the living room."

"All right," Emily said with a smile, feeling a little bit better already. "Maybe I just needed to have you here."

"Everything is easier when you don't feel like you're going at it alone. And you're never alone. Can we use these boxes?" Anita toed a couple of cardboard cartons sitting on the floor.

"That was the plan." At the time, Emily had felt that she was only cluttering up the room by putting the boxes in here, but now she was glad that she had them handy. She and Anita made quick work of packaging things up, although Emily had to remove Rosemary from the box several times. The cat kept digging around and pawing at this or that as though she was searching for something. "We'll have to leave the tops open to make it all fit, but I don't think that's a problem."

Anita followed her out to the garage. "It's not as though you'll take it over to the shop in this nasty weather, anyway."

A cool breeze blew through the open kitchen window as Emily opened the door to the garage. It sent a piece of paper fluttering out of the box she carried and drifting toward the kitchen floor. Rosemary snagged it midair before it could touch the linoleum.

"What did you find, silly girl?" Emily set her burden down on a kitchen chair while she retrieved the paper, figuring it was just some scrap that hadn't made it into the waste basket.

Her movements slowed when she realized that it was a familiar document. There was no mistaking the orange header with the logo for Phoenix Insurance. Emily had worked there long enough that she could probably draw that logo in her sleep. "What on earth?"

"A claim form?" Anita asked, peeking over her shoulder.

"Yes." Emily quickly scanned the information, but it didn't help her understand why this paper was here. "This would've been the sort of form that Sebastian would've worked with as an adjuster. It's for a fleet vehicle from Dorris Financial Consultants. They were always wrecking their cars."

"Then why do you look like you've seen a ghost?" Anita asked gently.

Emily stuck her tongue against the inside of her cheek as she continued to look over the document, looking for something that would make it make sense. "For one thing, this is Sebastian's handwriting up here at the top, with the number five and the question mark."

"That doesn't seem so unusual. You've been going through all of his things, and something like this would be bound to turn up," Anita said gently.

This wasn't about the emotional toll of seeing her late husband's handwriting, though. Not really. "In a way, yes. I've found all sorts of old receipts and shopping lists, but this form never should've left the office. It was supposed to be in the client's file. You know how Sebastian was always a stickler for the rules. He wouldn't have done something like that."

Anita shrugged. "Unless it was an accident. Even Sebastian, as perfect and wonderful as he was, probably made a mistake here or there. He could've accidentally mixed it up with other papers, brought it home, and misplaced it."

"I don't know." Emily wished she understood what was nagging at the back of her brain. Anita's suggestions were perfectly logical, and Emily couldn't let some silly form from a job where she no longer worked bother her so much. If she let herself get caught up in the emotions of it all, then she'd be right back where she was before she ever started going through his belongings. "You're right. It's not something I need to worry about. That claim would've been settled probably two years ago now. I'll just put it in the filing cabinet, and I can drop it off at Phoenix next time I'm going to be in that area."

"That's a girl," Anita said approvingly. "Now let's get these out to the garage. This box is getting heavy!"

"Right!" Emily set the claim form on the dining table and stepped into the garage.

CHAPTER SIX

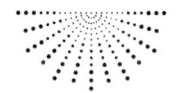

"Thank you for coming with me." The small cemetery on the outskirts of Little Oakley was a nice place for what it was, with a well-kept lawn, shade trees, and a pretty little chapel. It had been completely transformed over the span of a day, however. A massive array of white folding chairs had been put up in the largest, flattest area near the center of the graveyard. Raspberry pink bows decorated the back of each one. More pink ribbon had been set up as bunting on a podium at the front, and a large projector screen sat nearby.

Perhaps the largest transformation to the cemetery had been the sheer number of people. Cars lined the street in both directions as far as Emily could see, and she and Anita had been forced to park several blocks away. The chairs were nearly filled already, and she counted herself lucky that they were able to squeeze in near the back.

"You're very welcome," Anita returned as she seated herself next to a woman who was gabbing loudly on her cell phone with little regard to the fact that she was at a memorial service. She frowned. "I think it's safe to say you owe me."

"I do," Emily agreed. "I thought it only proper that I should attend the service. I didn't know Piper, but given the rest of the circumstances..." She rolled her hand through the air, not wanting to go into details in public about how she'd been the one to find the organizer's body.

Anita nodded. "I don't blame you a bit, but it's hard for me to imagine that there are truly this many people who actually did care about her. You said she came off as rude and arrogant."

"Shh!" Emily warned. "You're not supposed to speak ill of the dead."

"It's not as though she can hear us, darling," Anita reminded her. She leaned in closer. "And nobody could hear us over this loudmouth."

The woman next to her was still prattling away. "Oh, Molly, you just wouldn't *believe* how many people are here! It's like the whole town turned out and then some! I'm lucky I got here when I did, because it's down to standing room only. I think I see the news vans showing up, too. They'll be lucky to find any place to park, that's for sure! Well, you know, I was on her waiting list. Piper was going to do my master bedroom, and now I just don't know what I'm going to do!"

Anita rolled her eyes, but Emily wasn't surprised. However she'd managed it, and despite her abrasive personality, Piper had made herself into quite the star. The attendees were likely here for a number of reasons, whether they knew her personally, had used her services, or simply wanted to say they were there.

A sound at the microphone had them all turning their heads to the front. Nora Moss stood gazing out over the crowd, her chin angled up as she waited for the last bits of conversation to die down. "Thank you all so very much for coming. We're here today in memory of Piper Hawkins, a woman who had become near and dear to the hearts of Little Oakley. My name is Nora Moss, and I had the honor of growing up with Piper. I knew her before many of you did, and I want you to know that this little town was just as important to her as she was to it."

Emily was distracted as the man in the row in front of her leaned over to talk to his wife. "Why are we here again? Did you say this was a relative of yours?"

"No, you goose! This was the woman who helped me redesign the whole house! You know, all the library bookshelves, and the pantry, and the Christmas decorations in the basement?"

He nodded slowly. "Right."

"You never noticed," his wife grumbled.

"As you can see, this isn't your typical memorial service. Black is always the trend for these types of events, a color that's meant to respect the dead, but Piper always loved a nice bright pink." Nora ran her hand over the lapel of her own pink jacket and smiled. "She'd have been very happy to see just how much pink is represented here today."

"Funny, considering her office was all gray," Emily whispered.

"I'd like to start things off with a slideshow dedicated to Piper's life and all that she achieved. Please enjoy." Nora stepped aside and nodded to someone else. The projector screen illuminated with a smiling portrait of Piper as soft music played in the background. The woman next to Anita was filming everything on her cell phone, but nobody said anything to her about it.

In fact, as Emily looked around, there were quite a few people doing the same. It seemed shameful to her that an event such as this should be turned into a circus. Then again, from what she'd seen of her, Piper turned every event into a circus. She'd charged into Little Oakley Realty, which was already a busy place, and turned it completely upside down while she ordered all the cabinets emptied and the supplies inventoried. It was all put back together by the end, but that chaos had been required to get rid of the clutter and create some order.

The slideshow, which had included quite a few shots of the closets, drawers, and cabinets Piper had worked on, concluded. Nora stepped back up to her place at the podium. "Now I would like to invite any members of the community who would like to say something about Piper."

There was a general rustling through the crowd. Considering just how many people were here, Emily expected a line to form down the center row. One woman stood up and took the mic, but everyone else remained seated.

"I guess being popular online doesn't necessarily translate to being popular in real life," Anita noted.

Emily wanted to correct her, but Anita was right. Most of the crowd seemed more interested in participating simply because it was the social happening of the month and not because they cared about Piper. She didn't even see anyone crying.

"Thank you." As Nora once again took her place at the podium, Emily realized she hadn't been paying attention to what the other woman had said. There were no other volunteers who stood up. "Before we send Piper off with one final song, I want to make an announcement. While it's been a hard decision, The Happy Home will continue on."

Nora waited as a smattering of applause rippled through the audience. "Thank you. I know how hard Piper had worked on this business. It wasn't simply about having a job or making money. It was her purpose in life, something she knew she was destined to do. She had to fight hard to make it happen, and I know she wouldn't have wanted to see The Happy Home close its doors now that she's gone. It won't be quite the same, of course, but the rest of us will strive to make sure her legacy lives on. Thank you all for coming." She beamed a smile toward the audience as more music started playing.

"There you go," Anita said, nudging her with her elbow. "You can still hire someone to organize your closets."

Emily sighed. "Am I a bad person if I say I'm actually glad it wouldn't be Piper? She obviously knew what she was doing, but she just wasn't very nice. I'd hate to look in my nicely arranged linen closet and have it ruined by knowing someone hateful had done it. I'm not saying I'm happy she's dead," she added quickly. "I'm just happy that I won't have her in my home."

"You're allowed to feel that way," Anita decided. "It's your home, and you've worked hard to make sure there are as many positive memories there as possible."

Thinking of Sebastian, who was buried just up over the next hill, Emily nodded. "You're definitely right about that."

CHAPTER SEVEN

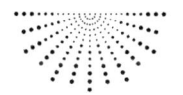

With her car finally empty of all her donations, Emily stopped by the market. With a bag of cat food and another one of litter, she headed over to Best Friends Furever and struggled through the door.

"Let me help you!" Lily Austin scrambled out from behind the front counter and around toward the door to take some of the load out of Emily's hands. She set both bags in the lobby chairs. "You bought the big ones this time."

Emily laughed. "It was all they had in stock. At first I thought that was just fine, since I hadn't brought any in for a while. I think next time I'll stick with the small bags." Her back was aching a little, but whether it was from her purchases or all the work she'd been doing at her home, she couldn't be completely sure.

"I can tell you with full confidence that the cats appreciate it. We've had a bit of a dip in donations lately, probably because everyone is off on their summer holidays and spending their money on flights and cruises. There's always something, but the animals still have to eat." Lily shook her head.

"Do you have a pet picked out for me this week?" Emily asked. "I'm definitely in need of some content for my blog, but the only other thing I've been writing about probably isn't a good idea at the time."

"I saw that you were working on your closets," Lily replied as she led the way behind the front counter.

"You've been reading it?" Emily was always flattered to know someone had bothered to click on her site, even if it was only for one post.

"Of course! It started out with just wanting to see what you posted about our shelter animals, but I enjoy everything you write. If you're interested in organizing, then I assume you know all about that Piper Hawkins getting killed. Well, I guess you'd simply have to be alive to be aware of it. The whole town has been talking." Lily opened the door into the dog kennel, where she was met with a cacophony of loud barking.

"I have." Emily had known Lily for a while now, and she'd gotten to know her better now that she'd been volunteering regularly at Best Friends Furever. The director was probably thirty years her junior, but Emily felt that they'd grown quite close. "To be honest, I had just done an interview with her for my blog a few days before she died."

Lily stopped by the cage of a large black dog and whirled around, her dark eyes wide. "Are you serious?"

"I am. I haven't decided if or when I'm actually going to post it, though. I feel a bit strange about the whole thing." Emily stopped and reached her hand in to pet the black dog, who wagged his tail excitedly. "It just feels wrong, even if I'm nice about it."

Now that they'd been in the kennel for a minute, the dogs were starting to calm down. Lily moved down to the end of the row and unlocked a cage. "I take it you didn't think Piper was very nice," she said with a little smirk.

"And I take it this is something you already know from experience," Emily noted. She crouched down as a big yellow Labrador came bounding out of the kennel. His fur was beginning to turn gray around his muzzle.

"Piper and I went to school together. She was always the popular one, and when she would tell us all about her plans to be rich and famous, we believed her." Lily grabbed a broom from a hook on the wall and swept out the dog's cage while Emily kept him occupied. "This is Amos, by the way. His owners moved and decided they couldn't take him along."

Distracted for the moment, Emily rubbed the big dog's ears. She looked into his liquid brown eyes and saw his big silly smile as he panted, and she simply didn't understand. "Why would anyone do that?"

Lily shrugged, and the lines at the corners of her mouth showed that she had heard this kind of story more times than she could count. "I haven't figured that out yet. Personally, I think the circumstances would have to be pretty extreme for me to give up a dog like Amos."

"Poor guy. Do you have any manners, Amos? Can you sit?" Emily pointed her finger downward.

The big dog immediately thumped his rear down onto the concrete.

"What a good boy you are! Do you like to play ball?" She grabbed a tennis ball from the box behind her and tossed it down the length of the kennel area. It was impossible not to grin as she saw him lope after it. While she couldn't possibly know everything about a given dog or cat just from spending a few minutes with them, she wanted to give her readers as much information as possible if they should decide to adopt.

"He's also great with kids and other dogs," Lily supplied. "We haven't tried him with cats yet, but I think he'd do just fine."

"At least his owners left him with you to make sure he could find another home," Emily replied as Amos dropped the soggy tennis ball directly into her hands. He wagged his tail as he waited for her to throw it again. "That's much better than leaving him behind."

"You're right." Lily stepped out of the cage to refill the dog's water bowl. "It's easy to judge someone, but it's probably far braver than most people think for them to come surrender him when they don't feel they can take care of him anymore."

Emily tossed the ball again, but this time she was ready with her cell phone. She snapped several shots of Amos as he came bounding back toward her. If she'd ever thought she wanted a dog, this sweet old guy would probably be it. As wonderful as he was, she couldn't quite tear her mind away from the subject it insisted on returning to time and again. "You said you knew Piper. What was it about her that made you think she really would be rich and famous?"

Lily made a face as she set the water bowl down. "She was the kind who decided what she wanted and went after it. When she wanted to be head cheerleader, she arrived early at practice and stayed late to prove her dedication. I think she might also have sabotaged a few of the other girls who were in the running. Then when she wanted Damian Hawkins for her boyfriend, she stole him right out from under the nose of Hope Clark."

"I see." Emily hadn't known Piper well or for very long, but those stories certainly did seem to fit her personality type. She gave Amos another scratch behind the ears when she realized she'd heard that name before. "Hold on a second. Damian Hawkins? As in her ex-husband?"

"That's the one. Come on, Amos." Lily put the big dog back in his kennel before moving over to the next one, which housed a little rat terrier mix. "Did you end up meeting him or something?"

This dog seemed more interested in taking a nap than in playing. Emily grabbed the broom and started on the floor while Lily cleaned the food and water bowls. "No, but I did overhear Piper having a rather nasty phone conversation about alimony, and I'm pretty sure I heard the name Damian."

"Yeah, that was him. He was handsome and smart, the kind of guy every girl that age swoons over. I honestly figured that Piper would ditch him at some point when she got tired of him, just because that was always what she seemed to do. They stayed together for quite some time, though, and married a few years after high school." The little rat terrier had awakened and was now looking pleadingly up at Lily. She reached in her pocket and gave him a treat.

Emily emptied the dustpan. "I wonder what happened between the two of them to make them hate each other so much. Well, I didn't hear his end of the conversation. Only hers."

"Who knows?" Lily said with a shrug as she refilled the dishes and put them back in the kennel. "Damian was some sort of financial hotshot, the kind of guy with a bunch of money and power. I heard he dragged their divorce out for quite some time instead of just signing on the dotted line and letting it go, but I guess that happens when you can afford a good attorney. It's a shame that anything has to be that way, if you ask me."

"I agree."

Lily straightened and leaned one hand on the wall. "You know, if I'm really honest, I think he did it."

"Damian?"

"I don't know all of what happened between them, but I'd be willing to bet it was a pretty toxic relationship. Piper may have stolen him away from Hope Clark, but Damian was the kid who got his parents to come in and talk the principal out of banning him from the championship football game when he'd been caught trying to steal the rival school's mascot. He was raised with the notion that he could bully anyone into doing what he wanted." She was frowning at the idea, but she smiled a little as she ruffled the little dog's ears.

Emily thought it was a pretty interesting theory. "Have you said anything to anyone about it?"

"Oh, no." Lily shut and locked the gate behind them as they moved to the next dog, a collie mix. "I'm sure everyone in Little Oakley is calling in their hunches, thinking they know what happened to Piper and wanting to earn their own few minutes of fame. I can't say I want to be a part of that."

"I can understand." Emily personally found the amount of people who'd shown up at the memorial service simply for the celebrity of it shameful, and she had no doubt people were finding other ways to do it as well.

And yet she couldn't stop thinking about the possibility that Damian Hawkins really did kill his wife. It followed her through the rest of her volunteer session as they chatted about the animals and the amount of supplies the shelter had on hand, and it lingered with her when she went out to her car.

The only thing she'd really thought about Piper's phone conversation at the moment was how rude it had been of her to carry it out right there in the middle of someone's workspace, but perhaps there was more to it than she'd realized. After all, hadn't Piper told her ex that he'd be paying her alimony until one of them was dead? Wasn't one of them dead now?

Nerves snaked in her stomach as Emily thought about the other implications behind this. Damian had a lot of money and influence, from what Lily had said. He'd been able to use it to make his divorce from Piper much harder on the both of them than it probably had to be. Could he have also used that leverage to have her killed so that he'd no longer have to pay alimony? It certainly seemed possible. She dialed Alyssa's private number.

"I'm afraid that's something we've already explored. Hang on just a moment." The detective constable was muffled for a few moments as she spoke to someone else. "I'm sorry. It's been an absolute madhouse in here over the past few days. Everyone has questions or suggestions about this case, and some civilians are claiming to be reporters just so they can try to get the news before anyone else does."

"I'm sorry to be contributing to that," Emily replied. "I don't mean to waste your time."

"You never could!" Alyssa insisted. "I always like hearing from you, and you're a wonderful resource of information. I'm just afraid that this time, we've already investigated Damian Hawkins. You weren't the only one who heard the two of them arguing. He was out of the country at the time, however, and it's all been verified."

"I see." Emily chewed her lip, torn between not wanting to push her friend on the police force too far but not wanting to leave out any piece of information that might help. "Is there any chance he could've hired someone to do it for him? And then of course he'd have the excuse that he wasn't in the area?"

Alyssa paused for a moment as she thought about it. "Possible, yes. Likely, probably not. I'm not going to say it won't be considered, but unless we get some solid evidence that points us in that direction, there's not much we can do about it."

"I suppose that's true." It wasn't as though they could look up a list of hit men in the local directory, after all. "You take care, Alyssa, and don't work too hard."

That particular clue was a dead end, but she had a feeling she'd find more.

CHAPTER EIGHT

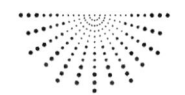

"All right. I think I'm finally getting the hang of this, Rosemary." Emily took off her raincoat and hung it up to dry. The thunder and rain had been incessant lately, with the day of the memorial service being just about the only one that'd turned out nice and sunny. She slipped out of her wellies and unwrapped the package she'd gone out to pick up.

The cat jumped up onto one of the armchairs to investigate more thoroughly. Her whiskers were constantly crazed and zigzagged no matter how often she groomed them, and the effect was enhanced as she wiggled her nose.

"It's a shadow box," Emily explained. "I may be trying to blog about organization and how to keep your home tidy, but there are people out there who know far more than I do when it comes to this stuff. I read an article recently that said if you really cherish something, you should find a way to display it instead of stuffing it away in a drawer or in the back of a closet. I think that makes a lot of sense, don't you?"

"Meow?" Rosemary asked.

"No, I won't be able to fit everything in here, but I think all of the important items will fit. Come on and let's find out." Emily carried the shadowbox to her bedroom, with Rosemary trotting along behind her. "Obviously, Sebastian's suit will simply have to stay in the closet. But look at this! All of the smaller things will fit in here just fine. Then I can have it all setting out and with far less dusting to do than if I tried to display them individually."

She opened the shadowbox and laid it out on the bed. Across the velvety back she arranged one of her favorite love letters from Sebastian. The poor man would be embarrassed if he knew there was any chance that someone else could read it, but this display was really just for her. One of his favorite books went in next, along with his wedding rings. Rosemary was right here next to her, contributing with curious looks, cute meows, and a stray hair or two.

"Now I just need his pocket watch!" Emily went back to the dresser drawer where she'd stashed all of her keepsakes as she'd gone through Sebastian's things, but it was empty. She checked the next drawer, and the next.

"Huh. Now that's very odd indeed." She tried to keep her alarm at a minimum, but it was building inside her chest. Sebastian had loved that pocket watch, and it'd been given to him by his grandfather.

"Rosemary, you didn't swipe it to play with the chain, did you?"

The cat looked up at her with her huge gold eyes and blinked slowly, claiming her innocence.

Emily nodded. "You're right. I wouldn't have left it out someplace where you could get to it. It's simply too special. Where else could it be?" She tapped her chin as she searched the room and tried to remember everything she'd done over the past couple of weeks. It was particularly difficult considering how much she'd moved around! As she checked various spots, Rosemary pawed around inside drawers, peeked under the furniture, and twirled around her ankles in support.

"I had it in the bedroom, but then I brought it out to the living room when I wasn't certain if one of the kids might want it. I meant to put it back in the bedroom, but I don't remember doing it. Oh, no!" Her exclamation made Rosemary jump, her tail fluffing out so that it looked like a bottle brush. "I must have accidentally taken it to the charity shop! I've got to go, Rosemary. You be a good girl!"

With her raincoat and boots right back on before they had a chance to dry, Emily raced across town to the Jenkins Foundation shop.

Inadvertently splashing through a puddle on her way inside, she swung open the door. The interior was cluttered with donated items to be sold for profits that might help the poor. Large racks of clothing took up most of the floorspace. Framed prints had been hung everywhere, while more of them rested in precarious stacks on the floor. Several shelves were laden down with books, vases, and other knickknacks.

Emily usually liked shopping in these sorts of places. It was fun to take her time as she rummaged through all the random items that'd been donated to find a treasure. She was often surprised at what people had been willing to give away, although now she'd done the same thing herself. Emily could only hope that she had gotten here soon enough and that someone hadn't already purchased the pocket watch.

"Can I help you find anything?" a friendly voice asked from behind the counter.

Emily opened her mouth to explain, but she paused as she realized she recognized the woman who'd spoken. She had thick dark hair pulled back into a low ponytail, and her wide eyes watched from behind glasses that constantly sagged a little on her nose. "Kyra, is it?"

"Do I know you, ma'am?"

"I'm sorry." What an awkward situation to explain! "I met you, in a way, when you were still with The Happy Home.

I was observing an organization project at Little Oakley Realty."

"Oh, right." Kyra made a face. "You were there when I got fired."

"I'm very sorry," Emily repeated. "I shouldn't have brought it up."

"No, that's all right," Kyra insisted. "I was trying very hard to stay focused on my work that day, so I'm afraid I'd hardly paid attention to you."

Emily hesitated, knowing that it must've been a very awkward situation for Kyra. Was it awkward enough for Kyra to come back to the office and murder Piper when she was working there alone? A former employee would certainly know what The Happy Home's schedule was like, and she'd definitely know where Piper would be in the building. "It wasn't right of her to fire you right there in front of everyone."

"Maybe not," Kyra shrugged as she arranged some teacups on a nearby shelf, "but I can't say it was unexpected. Piper had warned me several times about letting me go. What she didn't understand is that she was a very nerve-racking woman to work for! I never would've made so many mistakes if she wasn't breathing down my neck constantly. If I'm left to work on my own, then I do just fine. In a way, losing that job has been quite the blessing. Working here is much less stressful and far more satisfying. I like knowing that I'm doing something to help the poor instead of just seeing someone get their pantry tidied."

"I could see that." Emily pursed her lips. Kyra seemed like a nice girl, and she was happy now that she no longer worked for Piper. Did that mean she was innocent, or that she was just very good at covering up what she'd done? "There had to be some prestige that came with working for a company like The Happy Home, though, especially when you consider how popular the place had become."

"Pssht." Kyra made a derisive sound as she bent down to unpack more teacups from a box on the floor. "You would think so, but you'd be wrong. Piper worked us all like dogs. Worse than that, really."

Emily nodded. "I did notice that the rest of you were doing most of the work."

"That's because Piper was never really that much of an organizer in the first place." Kyra pushed her glasses up as she finished her little display. "She was far more about marketing and how she looks on social media. The looks were more important than the actual process, and she was always sweating bullets when it came time to start a new project because she never really knew how to go about it. She relied heavily on the rest of us, especially Nora."

"I don't understand." Emily skimmed the jewelry case nearby, remembering that Piper's murder wasn't at all the reason for her coming here. "If she wasn't any good at this sort of thing, why did she start a home organization company?"

"Because she could, I suppose, and because it was trendy. She wanted to take advantage of something that she thought would be big, and she did manage to do that. She was even getting ready to put out a book." Kyra shrugged, but then she leaned on the counter and looked at Emily seriously. "Do you want to know a secret?"

"Sure." Especially if it would lead her one step closer to finding out who had killed Piper Hawkins, although Emily wasn't yet completely convinced that it hadn't been Kyra.

The clerk glanced toward the front of the shop, but nobody else had come in. "Most of the photos Piper posted online were fakes."

"Fakes?" Emily repeated. "I don't understand."

Kyra nodded. "Piper would take a completely empty piece of space and fill it with all sorts of random junk, making it look as bad as possible. Then she'd have one of us empty it out again and arrange it with pretty bins, all in rainbow order or some such. She'd use these as before and after photos on her website, but they weren't real projects at all. We were all sworn to secrecy, of course, and it always drove me crazy that she should be able to get away with such a lie. I said something about it to her once, but she told me that was just the way business worked and everyone did it. I think that was why she didn't like me."

"I'm sorry to hear that." Emily had always worked hard when she was a secretary for Phoenix Insurance, and her manager had expected it, but never once had she felt mistreated or suspected that they were duping the public.

"Silly me." Kyra shook her head and wave her hand through the air as though to dismiss everything she'd said. "I'm sure you didn't come in to hear me complain about my former job. Is there something I can help you find?"

"I certainly hope so." Emily explained her mistake with the pocket watch. "I understand if you don't have it anymore, but I had to at least come down and take a look."

"A pocket watch?" Kyra stroked her chin. "Anything that comes in and might be of some value gets set aside for the manager to take a look at before it's priced. I can check around in back for you."

"That would be kind of you." Emily waited, trying to be patient. If she'd gone and lost Sebastian's pocket watch, then she'd regret ever starting this whole organization journey regardless of how much nicer her home was already looking.

In the meantime, she tried to distract herself by letting her mind return to Piper. Kyra could still very well have done it. Emily hadn't asked her for an alibi, nor had she outright accused her of murder. Kyra had the motivation, and she had the information to be able to carry it out. But would she really have done it? She was upset with Piper, but she hadn't so much as clenched a fist as she'd spoken.

"Is this it?" Kyra returned from the back with a pocket watch dangling from her hand.

"It is!" Emily exclaimed, not caring that her voice was far too loud for the quiet little shop. "Oh, you've found it! You've made my day! But what do I need to pay you to get it back?" She opened her purse, ready to dole out whatever the girl asked.

Kyra shook her head and held the watch out. "It was yours in the first place, and it's only right that you have it back. If you really want to give me something for it, then we can consider your time as sufficient payment. It was nice to chat with you and have someone who was willing to listen to my problems instead of just exclaiming how great Piper was."

"Thank you." Emily took the watch, knowing she would never make such a silly mistake again.

CHAPTER NINE

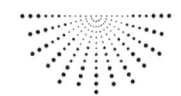

"Here's Gus! All ready to play!" Mavis put Gus's crate down on the floor and opened the door. The white cat eagerly paraded out. He paused and sniffed the air, knowing his friend was around here somewhere. He glanced to the left just as Rosemary attacked him from the right, batting him with the softness of her paws before taking off for the kitchen. He streaked after her.

Emily laughed. "They'll keep each other occupied for quite some time, I think."

"They always do." Mavis put the crate over in the corner to keep it out of the way. "I feel bad whenever we haven't been over here in a while, because I think he really enjoys having a playmate other than me. I do my best, but I'm just not as good as another cat."

"You could always adopt a second one. Lily has plenty of them down at the shelter. I just met a sweet little tuxedo cat named Annie the other day. She was sweet as pie, and Lily said she gets along well with other cats." Emily had truly enjoyed the time she'd been spending at Best Friends Furever, but it was hard to know there were so many pets who didn't have homes. She often found herself telling just about anyone who would listen about the plight of the homeless animals and suggesting that they go down and take a look. Combined with her blog features, she hoped she was making a difference.

"I'll keep it in mind, but I'd have to be sure that any new cat got along with Gus. I'd want them to be friends, with no chance of him feeling like someone is encroaching on his territory. Do you think Lily would allow a trial run, if I decided to do that?" Mavis watched as the two cats came tearing out of the kitchen and down the hallway.

"I imagine she would." Emily made a mental note to ask her the next time she was at the shelter. "Did you find a good spot for your father's hourglass?"

Her daughter smiled. "I sure did. I put it on my own desk at home. It seemed like a fitting place, and it keeps me from working too hard on any given thing. What about you? You've been putting in a lot of hard work on the house."

Emily sighed and ran a hand through her hair, realizing her wild curls had gone a little wilder than usual with all the extra humidity in the air. "Not as much as I'd like, and I keep getting distracted. It's this business with Piper Hawkins."

The cats sprinted back into the living room, this time with Rosemary in the lead. They made a turn around the end table before they took off again.

"I suppose Alyssa hasn't gotten it figured out just yet?"

Emily sighed as she got up and headed into the kitchen to start the tea kettle. "No, not yet. I know these things take time, and she's the professional. She and everyone else on the police force are doing everything they can to find a suspect. Part of the problem is that they're being completely inundated with phone calls and visits because it's such a high-profile case. I wouldn't be surprised if they end up having to hand it over to a higher authority."

Mavis had followed her, and she got the teacups out of a nearby cabinet. "Do they have any suspects?"

"I'm really not sure. They haven't released anything, and Alyssa hasn't had any time to talk." Emily poked around, decided which tea bags she wanted to use, and got them out.

"All right." Mavis put the sugar bowl on the kitchen table. "Do *you* have any suspects?"

The tea kettle whistled, and Emily poured the hot water over the bags. She thought for a moment before she answered, trying to organize her thoughts. There was always a lot to consider when something like this came up, and she didn't want to be one who jumped to conclusions. "Well, at first, I thought her ex-husband might've done it. The two of them had been arguing over alimony, and she insisted he'd keep right on paying it. I imagine some of that argument had to do with the fact that she was gaining such popularity, and he probably thought he shouldn't have to support her anymore, but that's just speculation."

Mavis sat down across from her mother as the cats finally settled down under the table, catching their breath as they cuddled up with each other. "But he didn't?"

"Probably not." Emily remembered that she wanted honey in her tea instead of sugar, so she returned to the kitchen to fetch it. "That was the one thing I was able to talk to Alyssa about, and she said he had a solid excuse. I'm not sure I buy it, since apparently he had plenty of money and influence. He could've just hired someone to do it."

"Who else?" Mavis pressed.

Emily studied her daughter. Mavis didn't have to ask if there was another suspect; she simply knew. It was nice that they could be this close without any sort of judgement between them. "There was an employee that Piper fired in a rather rude way. She seemed like a good next guess, and she certainly gave me plenty of dirt on her former employer, but I just have this feeling that it wasn't her."

"Your feelings have been right before." Mavis got up and headed into the living room.

"Where are you going?"

She returned a moment later with her laptop, and this time Mavis sat down next to her mother instead of across from her. "I had stopped by my office to grab my computer so I could work on a few things. I'm curious as to what this Piper Hawkins was like."

"You hadn't followed her online or anything?" The way that everyone else had talked about Piper, Emily imagined she was just about the only person in Little Oakley who *hadn't* already been part of her following.

"Not at all," Mavis replied with a shake of her head. "I just don't get into those sorts of things. Any interior designer would probably roll their eyes up in their head and pass out if they saw how plain and boring my apartment is. Here's her website. That wasn't hard to find."

Emily tapped her finger on the side of the computer. "Don't believe everything you see here. According to Kyra, the woman who'd been fired, she set up a lot of them to look like she'd done more work than she actually had."

"Like this one?" Mavis pointed to a supposed before-and-after shot of a linen closet. "I personally find it strange that someone would just happen to have all their towels coordinate quite that perfectly."

"I think that's exactly the sort of thing Kyra was talking about." Emily clicked her tongue. "I don't think I'd have given it a second thought before."

"What's this?" Mavis was now studying a photo of a handmade coffee mug with a drippy blue glaze.

Emily recognized it instantly. "That's the item that she claimed was her inspiration for the whole business. Yes, she's got the whole story there. I guess it hasn't been updated since her death, or maybe they're just going to leave it there in honor of her."

Mavis opened a new tab and began a search. "A person's website only tells the world what they want it to know. Let's see what else there is." She skimmed past all the initial links that went straight back to The Happy Home's website and social media pages.

"What's that one?" Emily brushed her foot over Rosemary's fluffy fur as she pointed to something that looked like a college newspaper.

"Hmm." Mavis quickly skimmed the article. "It looks like a feature that was done on her while she was still in school. It lists her as a marketing major."

"That explains how she was able to build up her clientele and reputation the way she did."

Mavis scrolled a little further down. "At the time this was written, she was interested in publishing."

Emily nodded. "Kyra said she was getting ready to release a book. I can only assume it was about organizing."

"But there isn't a single thing here that has to do with homes, organizing, interiors, or design. Obviously, people change their minds when they're young, and they don't always stick with what they initially think they're going to do, but it does seem like a pretty big switch."

Remembering what Kyra had said, Emily put her finger in the air. "If she was a marketing major, then she probably had a great sense for what people were going to like. Kyra theorized she was just taking advantage of a trend. And I do have to say, Piper's desk was much messier than I would've expected."

"Let's see what else there is. All of this is interesting, but it doesn't tell us anything concrete. You mentioned an ex-husband, so we can look up some information with a court records search." She tapped away on the keyboard and soon had a whole list of information on the screen.

"You can look all of that up?" Emily asked, astonished.

"Sure can. There's only so much information, but it at least gives us the basics. Here's a divorce from a Damian Hawkins. Down here there's another suit brought on by a Nora Moss. Then we have a traffic ticket."

"Wait, wait. Did you say Nora Moss?" Emily found the name on the screen, and she knew for certain this was one of the other women who worked for Piper. "What's that about?"

"It says copyright infringement, but the case was thrown out due to lack of evidence," Mavis said once she'd clicked on it. "There's no more information than that."

"That's certainly interesting." Emily's brows drew together as she tried to think. "Why would two people continue to work together if there'd been a lawsuit between them? And why would Nora be suing her for copyright infringement?"

"Maybe we can find out." Mavis opened yet another tab and tried to search for more information on the case. "I was hoping for a newspaper article or something, but whatever happened, they were able to keep it hush-hush. Do you think this Nora had anything to do with it?"

Emily sighed. "I'm starting to think that anything is possible. It could've been Nora, or maybe it was some client who hired Piper and was unhappy that she wasn't the one who personally rolled up her sleeves and got the work done. It's getting frustrating!"

"Don't stress yourself over it so much." Mavis closed out her tabs and shut the laptop. "We should be using our time together in a better way. Why don't you show me how your closets look?"

CHAPTER TEN

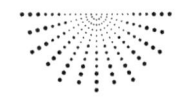

Two days later, Emily knew exactly what she needed to do. There was less clutter in her home than there'd been a few weeks ago, but it still didn't look as wonderful as all the amazing arrangements she'd seen online. No matter how hard she tried, and no matter how much she was inspired by wanting to blog about it, Emily just couldn't seem to make it happen.

That was exactly why she found herself driving back over to the very scene of the crime. The Happy Home looked just as bright and cheerful as it'd been the last time she'd come here. The biggest difference was that the crowd of squad car chasers had dissipated, and it looked like any other business at this point. The riot of flowers in the front of the building had thrived with all the rain and had shot forth a brand-new set of blooms.

A beaming receptionist now sat at the front desk. She wore the raspberry pink polo that was the uniform of the business, and her lipstick matched. "Hello, and welcome to The Happy Home! How can I help you?"

She was nervous for many reasons, not the least of which was the fact that she had no idea just how much this was going to cost her, but she'd already made the commitment to do this, and since she was standing here, there was no turning back. "My name is Emily Cherry, and I have an appointment with Nora."

"Let me just check the schedule." Tapping raspberry pink nails that matched her shirt and lipstick, she consulted her computer. "Wonderful! You're right on time, and we always appreciate that around here. I'll take you back to see Ms. Moss."

Escorting Emily down the hallway, she knocked softly on the doorway of the blue office Emily had peeked into briefly when she'd been here before. "Mrs. Cherry is here to see you, ma'am."

"Mrs. Cherry, how very nice to see you today." Nora stood up from her desk. She wore a fitted suit in the same berry-colored shade as everything else around here, and she smiled brightly as she came forward to shake Emily's hand. "I was a bit surprised to see you on the schedule. Please have a seat and tell me what we can do for you."

"Well, I've been thinking a lot about your company," Emily began. She glanced around the office, noting just how different in style it was from Piper's down the hall. The walls were painted a beautiful shade of robin's egg blue that contrasted pleasantly with the vintage rolltop desk. Other vintage cabinets with glass doors had been hung on the wall where they showed off a collection of milk glass. Everything was neat as a pin and perfectly arranged, making it look like something straight out of a magazine, but Emily supposed that was exactly the look a place like this was going for. On a shelf all to itself over on the right sat the lopsided coffee mug with the drippy blue glaze that Emily had seen before in Piper's office. "My, but your office is beautiful!"

"Thank you. I designed it myself," Nora replied with a smile.

"Anyway." Emily cleared her throat. "I had initially started speaking with Piper because I wanted to interview her for my blog, but I realized I could also use her help when it came to sorting out my home. All of that got put on the back burner, for obvious reasons, but as I've tried to do it all myself, I've realized that I could still use some help."

"Splendid! And I'm pleased that you decided to come straight to me, but of course you didn't have to. Any one of our very talented staff would be able to help with an estimated cost of our services. Perhaps you could tell me a little bit about your home, and that would be a starting point. We do usually like to come out and see the home for ourselves to get the best gauge of what's needed." She held a pink pen at the ready.

"Now, I don't want to push you too far," Emily replied. "I know that things have likely been very stressful around here now that Piper is gone, and I'm sure the publicity has made things difficult as well. If you need to put me at the end of a list, then I completely understand."

"There's no need for that," Nora responded with a flick of her wrist. "We're doing quite well."

"I think it's just wonderful that you've decided to carry on the torch in her memory." Emily was here to get a bid for services, yes, but she was also here to get much more. She stood up and wandered over to the little display near the window, pointing at the coffee mug on its little shelf. "I recognize this. What a fitting tribute. There are so many people these days who would simply take the opportunity to swoop in and grab all the profit, knowing that the publicity from Piper's death would bring a lot of free advertising to the business."

Nora's smile wavered slightly. "That would be terrible."

"But I know it's not like that around here. Everyone cares about each other, and it's just wonderful." Emily waved her arms around to encompass the business and all the people who worked there. Her elbow knocked straight into the mug. It tumbled off the little shelf toward the floor. Emily's heart clenched as she realized what she'd done, but her arms darted forward. She couldn't say what made her reflexes suddenly work as they did, but she was relieved when her hands closed around the cold clay.

"That was close!" she breathed, standing perfectly still lest she accidentally let go of it again.

Nora was on her feet, her hands reaching out through the air. "A little too close," she replied, her voice shaking.

The mug in Emily's hands was turned upside down. She started to right it to put it back on the shelf, but then she noticed the initials carved into the bottom. It wasn't strange at all that a child at summer camp would put her initials on something she'd made. It *was* strange that the initials were NM. Emily frowned. "I have a feeling that there's a much bigger story behind this mug than that it was the beginning of an entire company."

With another shaking breath, Nora slowly sat down. "I'm afraid I don't know what you're talking about. I'd like you to put that back, please."

Emily did as she was asked, but then she moved over and leaned against the back of the chair in front of Nora's desk. "I know there's something happening here, Nora, and it must be something very painful for you judging by the look in your eyes. I also know that you and Piper have a history beyond being best friends, and beyond being coworkers. Something else happened, something that made you decide to take her to court. That couldn't have been easy." She might just be chasing another wild goose, but she had to know.

Nora looked down at her hands where they were folded on her desk. "Piper and I really were best friends, back in college. She was majoring in marketing, and she was so into it that she practically lived and breathed it. I had an idea for a business, and I brought it to her because I knew she'd be able to tell me whether or not it was a good idea."

Now Emily sat down again. "Organizing homes for people," she said gently.

"That was it." She paused, and for a moment Emily wasn't sure she was going to continue. "It was a passion of mine. I'd helped a few friends move and things like that, and I realized it was something I was really into. I just didn't know if it was actually a viable business plan, so I brought it to Piper. She knew about these kinds of things."

"What did she say?" Emily couldn't help it. Her heart went out to Nora when she saw all the years of pain written on her face.

Another sigh escaped. "That it was ridiculous. It would never work, and if it did, it would only be for a short time. The next thing I knew, she was starting up the business herself. She claimed it was entirely her idea."

Emily pointed at the wall. "What about the coffee mug?"

"Mine, from one of my summers at camp. I don't think Piper probably ever went to camp. She actually went to the charity shop where I'd donated a bunch of things I was getting rid of just to buy it. I know now she only did it because she wanted to create a story behind the business, and she knew that some handmade item would pull at people's heartstrings." Nora ran a hand through her dark blonde hair, mussing it.

"So, you sued her."

"Yes. It made sense at the time, but I didn't have any way of proving that I'd actually come up with the idea before she did. Just the idea of an organizing company wasn't unique enough, so I showed the judge all the notes and drawings I'd made. I couldn't prove that I'd made them before Piper had opened The Happy Home, hence there was no case to be made at all." Nora looked completely defeated, her shoulders hunched forward. "When things started to really pick up steam here, I just couldn't stand the thought of her taking everything that I'd worked for and turning it all to her own advantage."

"You know," Emily said quietly, "I know someone on the police force. She's a very smart detective constable, but she's also very kind. I'm sure she can work with you and help you. I'll give you her number if you'll call right away."

Nora turned in her chair to look out the window. A series of expressions raced over her face, everything from relief to sadness to anger. Finally, she looked back at Emily. "I'll do that. Thank you."

"I just have one other question to ask you," Emily said as she looked in her purse for Alyssa's business card. Why did you come work for Piper if she'd stolen your idea? That had to be hard on you."

Nora let out a small, wry laugh. "You're not wrong there. It seems crazy, I'm sure. But I truly love organizing. It's something I'm good at, but marketing is something Piper was really good at. There was no way I could open my own company and compete with her, so the next best thing was to work for her. At least I'd know I had a job in a field I enjoyed, although I can see now what a mistake that was."

Emily nodded. "We all make mistakes sometimes, dear. It's how we handle them that counts."

CHAPTER ELEVEN

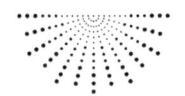

"We can put all of the beads in these little containers I picked up, and then they won't spill."

"Save one for the buttons, as well."

"How do you want to be able to find your books? Alphabetical by author, or that thing where they're arranged by the color of the cover?"

"That's ridiculous! Make them alphabetical!"

"Watch out for Rosemary!"

Emily's house was complete chaos, but at least it was chaos in a different way than it had been. Mavis, Phoebe, and Anita had all shown up on her doorstep that morning, soaked to the bone but ready to pitch in and put the finishing touches on the closets. The three of them didn't always agree on exactly how it should be done, but she could certainly see that they were doing for her what she hadn't been able to do for herself. Boxes and bags were moved from room to room, with shouts of suggestions and questions called after them. A small donation pile had been started once again as more unneeded items were unearthed. Emily darted around as busily as her cat did, trying to keep track of it all and wondering how it was possibly going to come together.

"Come get a photo of this shelf for your blog," Mavis encouraged, pulling her into the living room. Thunder rumbled outside the windows, but nobody was paying it any attention. "I think it looks really good, and your readers might really appreciate it."

"I'll do it, but only if you let me give you all the credit. It looked terrible before you arrived." Emily got out her cell phone and clicked a few pictures, trying to think of just how she was going to word the post that would go with it. This particular part of her home hadn't been a part of her original goal, but the more she'd cleaned, purged, and sorted, the more spots she found needed improvement. What had once looked like a very random assortment of knickknacks now looked like a purposely curated collection.

Mavis laughed. "You do what you want to with it. It's your blog, after all, and I imagine you have plenty of content for it now."

Emily tilted her head to one side. "Well, that's mostly true. I think my journey with organizing has been an important one, and it's one that people may find helpful. They need to know that it's just not always as easy as others make it look on the internet or on TV, but that doesn't mean it isn't worthwhile. It's just going to take more time and effort than you think!" she laughed.

"I don't know," Mavis replied, nodding at her sister where she sat on the floor near the fireplace. "Phoebe has only just started, and look what she's already done with the bookshelves. They look better than what you'd find in a library."

"It wasn't that much work," Phoebe protested as she stood up and dusted off her knees. "Books are easy, anyway. They look nice on their own, even if you don't do some sort of special scheme with them. Besides, I was a good candidate for that since I'm already used to crawling around on the floor with my kids."

"Better you than me," Emily agreed as she took photos of the bookshelf as well. This was an area where she hadn't decided to get rid of very many things, but a little bit of cleaning and repositioning had gone a long way. Emily hadn't realized just how much dust had accumulated on the tops of the books where she couldn't see it. "You spent an awful lot of time down on the floor, sorting them all and dusting them off!"

Phoebe hugged her. "I was happy to do it."

"Come see what you think!" Anita called from down the hall.

When they joined her, she stood proudly in front of the closet door with her chin up and a cat's smile on her face. "Keep in mind that I'm no professional. I haven't really done a lot of research to find out how most people are doing things. I just went with my instincts, and I thought it worked. If you don't like it, Emily, then I won't be offended in the slightest when you rearrange it a different way."

"Just show me!" Emily cried, so excited she could barely stand it. Anita was neat and organized in her life in many ways, and Emily was sure that whatever she'd done with the closet would be fantastic.

Anita whipped open the door to reveal an array of elegantly folded towels on the top half of the shelves. The very top shelf that was hard to reach held all the miscellaneous items that nobody had a clue what to do with, and they were neatly packed away in pretty boxes. Toward the bottom, Anita had wrangled all of Emily's craft supplies. They were categorized, labeled, and stacked so beautifully that Emily didn't know if she'd ever want to touch them again for fear of messing them up.

"I think *you* should open your own business," Emily enthused as she looked through it all.

"I'll be your second client," Phoebe said. "This looks much better than the bookshelves."

Mavis nodded. "Count me as your third! Maybe you could come give my boring apartment some style."

"Now, now." Anita waved off their compliments, but she was beaming. "That's all very flattering, but I think I'd go nuts if I tried to do this for a living. It's one thing to do it for yourself or for someone you know very well, but for complete strangers? I wouldn't dream of it."

Emily nodded, thinking about Nora and Piper. Nora had all the know-how when it came to home organization, and Piper was incredibly intuitive when it came to marketing. If only the two of them had been able to put their heads together in the first place, The Happy Home might still be a thriving business. As it was, the residents of Little Oakley would have to make their own closets and pantries look nice now that the place had been shut down. The whole thing had been such a shame, but it was nice to know that justice would be served.

"I can't say that I blame you," she said to Anita. "Maybe the better thing would be for us all to promise to help each other when we get behind. This is so much more fun when you have company!"

"What about the shadow box?" Phoebe asked. "You said you were doing something special for Dad's things."

"Right this way." Recovering Sebastian's pocket watch from the charity shop had been such a relief, and Emily had placed it in the shadow box right away. It now hung on the wall with a framed photo of Sebastian on one side and their wedding photo on the other.

"It's absolutely perfect, darling," Anita said as she looped her arms through Emily's.

"Yes, definitely," Phoebe agreed.

"I think he'd be very flattered," Mavis added.

Emily pulled in a deep breath and let it go, grateful to be surrounded with so much love and support. "I miss him terribly, but having the chance to go through everything he'd left behind allowed me to work through some of that. I can let go of some of my emotions surrounding his death just as I could let go of some of his belongings, but the most important part of it all will be right here." She patted her hand over her heart.

∽

THANK YOU FOR CHOOSING A PUREREAD BOOK!

We hope you enjoyed the story, and as a way to thank you for choosing PureRead we'd like to send you this free Special Edition Cozy, and other fun reader rewards...

Click Here to download your free Cozy Mystery PureRead.com/cozy

Thanks again for reading.

See you soon!

OTHER BOOKS IN THIS SERIES

If you loved this story and want to follow Emily's antics in other fun easy read mysteries continue **dive straight into other books in this series...**

Read them all...

A Troubling Case Of Murder On The Menu

A Crafty Case Of Murder At The Fair

A Hairy Case of Murder At The Animal Sanctuary

OUR GIFT TO YOU

AS A WAY TO SAY THANK YOU WE WOULD LOVE TO SEND YOU THIS SPECIAL EDITION COZY MYSTERY FREE OF CHARGE.

Our Reader List is 100% FREE

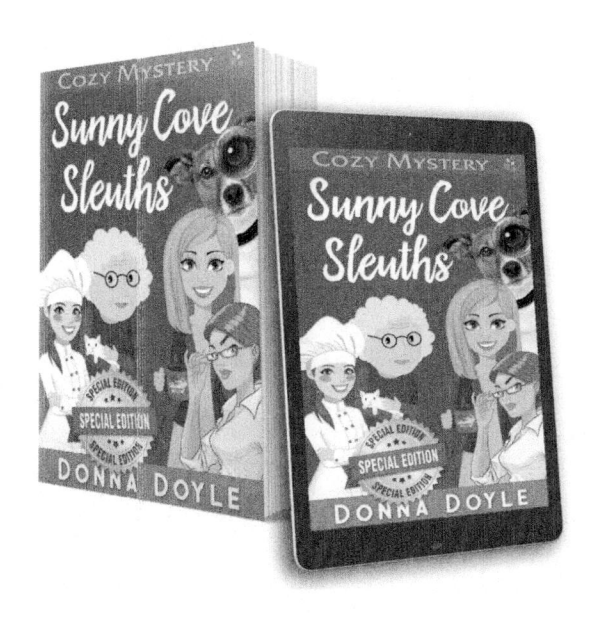

Click Here to download your free Cozy Mystery
PureRead.com/cozy

At PureRead we publish books you can trust. Great tales without smut or swearing, but with all of the mystery and romance you expect from a great story.

Be the first to know when we release new books, take part in our fun competitions, and get surprise free books in your inbox by signing up to our Reader list.

As a thank you you'll receive this exclusive Special Edition Cozy available only to our subscribers...

Click Here to download your free Cozy Mystery
PureRead.com/cozy

Thanks again for reading.
See you soon!

Printed in Great Britain
by Amazon